Silly Tillie

Written and illustrated by Jeanine Wine

Good Books
Intercourse, PA 17534

Silly Tillie
Copyright © 1989 by Good Books, Intercourse, PA
17534
International Standard Book Number: 0-934672-62-8
Library of Congress Catalog Card Number: 87-38311

Library of Congress Cataloging-in-Publication Data
Wine, Jeanine M.
  Silly Tillie / written and illustrated by Jeanine Wine.
    p.   cm.
  Summary: The owner of a laundromat is unsym-
pathetic to the needs of Silly Tillie, a homeless person in
the neighborhood, until one day when he needs her
help.
   ISBN 0-934672-62-8 : $12.95
  [1. Homeless persons—Fiction.] I. Title.
PZ7.W7248Si 1989
[E]—dc 19
                        87-38311
                           CIP

When people looked at Silly Tillie they usually made a face.

Her hat had been watered by many rains and some said more than plastic flowers grew there.

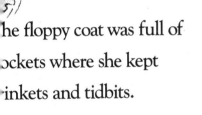

he floppy coat was full of
ockets where she kept
inkets and tidbits.

Tillie pushed along a rusty cart holding everything she called her own.

Home was wherever they could be together.

In the winter, Silly Tillie thought about the Super
Scrub Laundromat where eight deluxe dryers blew
clouds of warmth into the air.
She would try to huddle in their heat to melt the
shell of snow that covered her. But if Mr. Slotman,
the owner, saw Tillie, he would yell, "Get away,
you're not wanted here."

Once he even overturned the cart and shoved Tillie away, making her fall and tear her stockings.

When the grey frozen night brought chilling winds, Tillie would find a sheltered nook where she could make a tent out of beaten-up boxes and newspapers. Her stomach would rumble and growl.

By morning, Tillie was so hungry that she thought she could hear breakfast being made in kitchens all across the neighborhood.

There was the hiss of five-hundred and seventy-five eggs slipping into hot butter, the jingle of cereal hitting seven-hundred and eighty-two bowls, and the thug thug thug of milk being poured into tall glasses. All the clanging of spoons and forks on bowls, plates and tabletops made Tillie's head throb.

Her breakfast was an old hot dog roll she found in a trash can near
Seventeenth Street. Nibbling hungrily, she thought about Mr. Slotman and
the Super Scrub laundry.

Mr. Slotman offered a free cup of coffee to all his customers, but he never offered one to Silly Tillie. He said he could not afford to give coffee away to someone who slept out of doors and smelled like a pile of dirty old laundry.

One night, after all the neighborhood stores had closed and only the streetlights remained awake, Mr. Slotman emptied the change from the eight deluxe dryers and sixteen washing machines. He put the money in a green metal box and wrapped it tightly with his arm.

As Mr. Slotman clicked the lock of
the alley door, a stranger grabbed the
cashbox and started kicking and
punching Mr. Slotman and knocking
him in the head!

Mr. Slotman listened as the ching
chang clang of the cashbox and the
tap pat pat of the thief's heels grew
softer and softer in the distance. As
hard as he tried, Mr. Slotman could
not get up.

When the sun started to stretch and yawn in the eastern sky, Mr. Slotmar still lay bruised and bleeding in the alley.

Maria, who ran a bakery, was carrying out garbage when she saw someone curled up near the laundry. She was going to go over and have a look, but ran inside when the first batch of cookies started to burn.

A teacher taking a shortcut to school
saw Mr. Slotman,

and so did the man from the electric company who came to make some repairs.

In fact, quite a few people passed by Mr. Slotman that
morning —
and not one of them stopped to help.

Then a lumpy, bumpy lady, playing hide-and-go-seek with the wind,
wheeled her cart into the alley. She began rooting through trash in hopes
of finding something warm to wear. Silly Tilly spied what looked like
crumpled-up clothes lying near the laundry.

Like an old pirate digging for treasure, Tillie bent over to scoop up her precious find. But then she saw this was not a pile of laundry.

It was Mr. Slotman!

She also saw Mr. Slotman's cap, coat and mittens.

Silly Tillie tugged at those mittens so
hard, that when they finally popped
from Mr. Slotman's fingers, Tillie
reeled backwards and landed on the
ground with a bump!

She stretched those silky mittens over
her sandpapery hands. Only a very
fine lady wore mittens such as these!

Tillie unbuckled the hat and jerked. Off it came, roughly pulling Mr. Slotman's head.

This was a grand hat. It was lined with fleece as soft as a kitten, and it was covered with wool so thick that not a flake of snow could work its way inside.

The coat was next. The wind would never find her in that coat!

Just then Mr. Slotman moaned. His lips were already turning a little purple, like Tillie's lips when she had to spend a whole day crouching in a wet winter alley.

His fingers were curling into a fist, trying to warm themselves against each other. Silly Tillie knew what that was like.

Slowly Tillie took the hat and put it back on Mr. Slotman's head. She pulled his mittens back on too, more gently this time.

Then she ran through the alley and into the street yelling, "We need some help here, we need help!"

But everyone she turned to just made
a face.

Out of breath from shouting, Tillie came back to Mr. Slotman's side.

Somehow she managed to help him into the cart.

Tillie pushed and puffed as hard as she could. The hospital was five whole

blocks away and Mr. Slotman needed a Doctor fast!

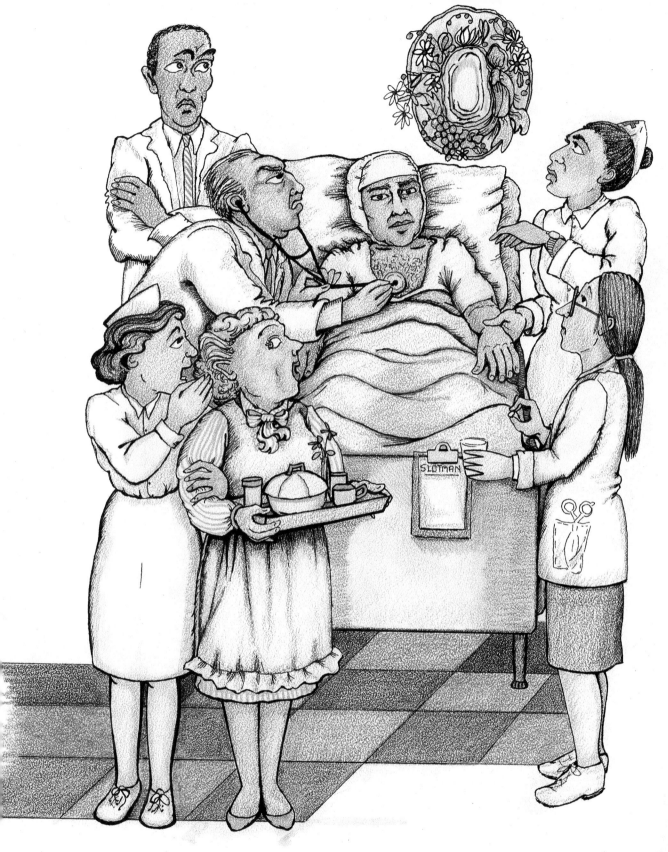

Everyone wondered how Mr. Slotman got that hat! It was made of soggy straw, was decorated with sticky plastic flowers, and smelled a little like wet skunk.

But Mr. Slotman hung it over his bed and would not let anyone even think about moving it.

To Mr. Slotman it was the brightest, most colorful, sweetest-smelling hat that he had ever seen!